Mr. Banks
Is Moving

Fulton Books, Inc.
Meadville, PA

Published by Fulton Books 2020

ISBN 978-1-64654-434-9 (paperback)
ISBN 978-1-64654-435-6 (digital)

Printed in the United States of America

Mr. Banks Is Moving

DONNA FORREST GORSICK

Chapter One

"I guess I'll have to move," fussed Mr. Banks. "Every day the same thing—loud noises, brakes squealing, and horns blowing. It's enough to drive anyone crazy!"

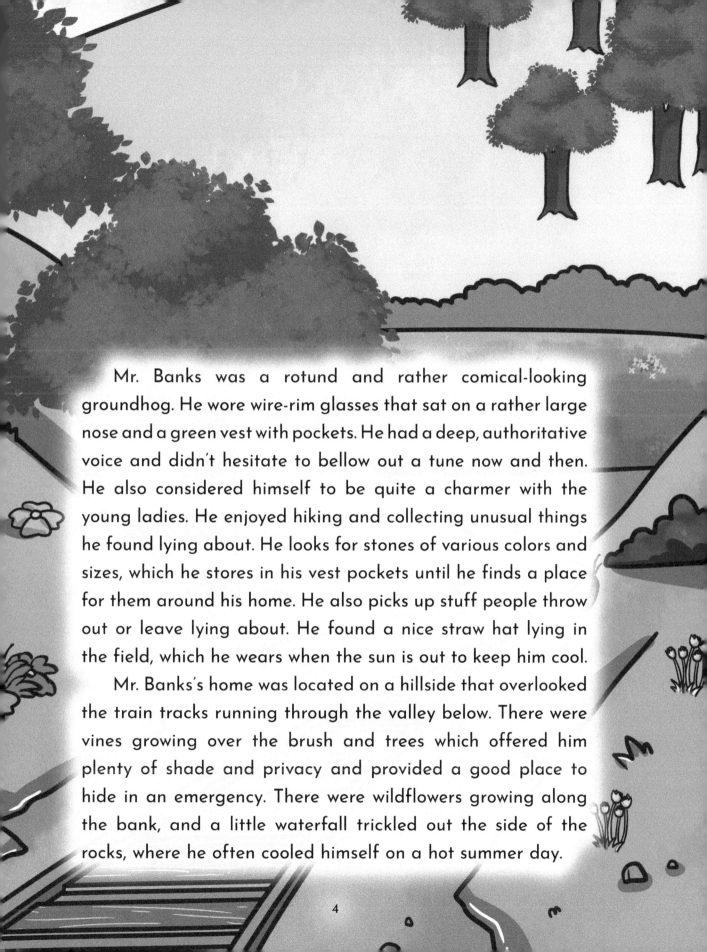

Mr. Banks was a rotund and rather comical-looking groundhog. He wore wire-rim glasses that sat on a rather large nose and a green vest with pockets. He had a deep, authoritative voice and didn't hesitate to bellow out a tune now and then. He also considered himself to be quite a charmer with the young ladies. He enjoyed hiking and collecting unusual things he found lying about. He looks for stones of various colors and sizes, which he stores in his vest pockets until he finds a place for them around his home. He also picks up stuff people throw out or leave lying about. He found a nice straw hat lying in the field, which he wears when the sun is out to keep him cool.

Mr. Banks's home was located on a hillside that overlooked the train tracks running through the valley below. There were vines growing over the brush and trees which offered him plenty of shade and privacy and provided a good place to hide in an emergency. There were wildflowers growing along the bank, and a little waterfall trickled out the side of the rocks, where he often cooled himself on a hot summer day.

He had an excellent view of the area. There was a hill on the other side of the railroad track that led up to a wooded area on the left and an open field on the right. The field stops at the edge of the highway where Mr. Banks would often sit in the shade under a bush, and watch the children play in the playground across the road. They were so full of energy and seemed to have such fun. Mr. Banks chuckled to himself just thinking about it.

He would watch the cars pass by taking people to work, school, and church or wherever they were going. He had thought it was the perfect place to live and use to consider himself very lucky to have found such a nice location.

Now he was considering moving. The one thing he hadn't counted on was the area growing so quickly.

Chapter Two

The once-peaceful place he called home had become a sea of strange faces, new businesses and new homes.

Almost every morning there would be a traffic jam with horns blowing and brakes squealing. Not to mention the continuous flow of fumes that floated over his home like a cloud, making him cough and choke.

Mr. Banks used to enjoy hearing the whistle blow as the train occasionally passed by his home. But now, it would rumble past at all hours, blowing its whistle and causing everything in his home, including him, to shake. He couldn't get any sleep. He was at the end of his rope and had to do something.

Mr. Banks decided he would move to a nice wooded area he spotted across the road, behind the church. It was far away from all the noise and fumes and he would finally be able to get some rest.

Chapter Three

Now that he made his decision, all he had to do was pack up his belongings in his backpack and take off. He didn't have a lot of stuff, so moving wouldn't be too big of a job.

He figured he would have to hike down the hill, cross the railroad tracks, climb back up the other side, cross four lanes of traffic, and cross the parking lot to the playground. From there, it was a short walk into the woods. *I can do that,* he thought to himself.

Mr. Banks half walked, half skidded down the side of the hill where he lived. Having reached the bottom with only a couple of scratches to his knees, he stood beside the railroad track looking in both directions. All he had to do was hop over the rails, one at a time, until he reached the other side. A *piece of cake*, he thought.

He hopped over the first rail dragging his backpack behind him. He had only taken a couple of steps when he felt the ground vibrating. A train was coming!

Mr. Banks started to run only to find the strap to his backpack was stuck on the edge of the track. He pulled and pulled trying to free the strap. He didn't have much but would like to keep what he had.

The train was getting too close, and Mr. Banks was frantic.
He had to get off the track.

The train blew its whistle, and he could see the train getting closer and closer. He made one final jerk on the bag, and it came free, causing Mr. Banks to fly over the other side of the track, barely in time to keep the train from hitting him.

He was so frightened he couldn't move. He was sprawled out in the grass looking up at the sky, waiting for his heart to slow down and his legs to quit shaking, before he continued his journey.

When Mr. Banks was able to stand without his legs wobbling, he started climbing the hill to get to the road. Although the hill didn't seem very steep when he came down it, going up was a little more challenging. Mr. Banks considered himself to be in good physical condition, but climbing even a small hill in the August heat was unbearable, and he didn't consider this to be a small hill.

When he reached the top of the hill, he found a cluster of bushes close to the road where he could rest and feel a refreshing breeze from the passing cars.

While resting in the shade, Mr. Banks was thinking about the best way to cross four lanes of this busy road and survive it. He watched for a few minutes and noticed that there were several breaks when there were no cars traveling in either direction. If he timed it just right, he could cross all four lanes quickly and get safely to the other side.

As usual, there was one thing Mr. Banks didn't count on. He picked up his backpack and watched in both directions. When it was clear there were no cars coming, he took off running across the road. He ran across the first two lanes, onto the median, and when he got about halfway across the second set of lanes, he looked up, and to his horror, a big dump truck had turned on the road he was crossing and was almost on top of him.

He didn't have time to do anything but curl up in a little ball in the middle of the road, as he was sure this monster was about to run over him. The truck passed right over Mr. Banks without touching a hair on his head. When he realized he was still alive, he got up and ran across the road and down the hill to the church parking lot, never looking back. All he could think about was getting to a safe place.

Chapter Four

Mr. Banks flopped down in the grass and took a deep breath. The hard part was over. He survived and was almost to the woods where he would look for his new home. The rest would be a breeze. He looked around to see where he was and realized he was at the edge of the parking lot by the church, where he watched the children play. He just needed to cross the parking lot to get to the woods.

22

Again, Mr. Banks didn't count on one thing. He was about to collide with several curious youngsters coming out of the church to play. The first hint of trouble came when he saw one boy pointing at him and yelling to the other kids. The next thing he knew, a bunch of kids were running toward him.

Mr. Banks looked around and ran toward the parking lot and hid under a car. He was perfectly still, not making a sound, hoping they wouldn't find him. No such luck. First, one face, then another, peeked under the car at him. One of the kids grabbed a stick and tried to poke him while another was yelling at the top of his lungs hoping to scare him into running out.

By now Mr. Banks was tired and quite angry. *Enough is enough*, he thought. He turned toward the children and gave them his fiercest look and growled ferociously. They all jumped back, startled at his sudden aggressive behavior. Mr. Banks knew he wouldn't harm them, but they didn't seem so sure. They backed away and decided it would be more fun to play on the swings and slide. Mr. Banks watched them return to the playground and, for the last time that day, grabbed his backpack and ran toward the woods.

Chapter Five

Mr. Banks walked until he came upon a creek winding through the woods. He took a refreshing drink of water and sat down on a big rock to rest and think about all that had happened to him that day. He sat there for a long time then got up to search for his new home.

He found a hollow stump surrounded by flowers and vines. He could smell honeysuckle and hear the creek flowing over the rocks. What he didn't hear was the noise from the highway or feel the rumbling of the train as it passed, but could hear the whistle blow in the distance. Satisfied, he decided this would be the place to make his home.

Mr. Banks unpacked the few possessions he had in his backpack and placed them inside the hollow stump along with the pine needles he had gathered to make a nice soft bed.

Exhausted from the days' events, Mr. Banks curled up on his new bed and soon fell to sleep listening to the lullaby of the crickets singing and the water trickling gently over the rocks.

Tomorrow, he would find some new friends and have new adventures.

About the Author

Donna is married with two children and one grandchild. She and her husband are now retired.

Writing has been a hobby of hers for many years. However, working full-time didn't leave many extra hours in the day to get her stories to the publishing stage.

Now that she has retired, she has more time to devote to her writing. She hopes her stories encourage the children who may read them to engage their imaginations and enjoy the adventures of the characters she writes about.